Pieces

of/by

Dr. Vandana Pathak

First Published in February 2023

ISBN: 978-93-5741-199-8

BLUEROSE PUBLISHERS

www.BlueRoseONE.com

info@bluerosepublishers.com

+91 8882 898 898

Cover Design:

Muskan Sachdeva

Typographic Design:

Rohit

Distributed by: BlueRose, Amazon, Flipkart

Foreword

The poems in this book, like the author, are on a journey that isn't fixed by the outside world and its limitations. Having known a little about the artist's life I can see her walk down a mountain road in Himachal Pradesh, grapple with the idea of commitment and relationships the way society sees them, delve into understanding what being a woman means to her as an individual and also as part of society and a family unit and being a poet.

Phases of her life are mirrored. A rebellion against shackles is reflected. But more than anything else, a refusal to be placed into any effective limitation and yet an acceptance of deeper emotional intense relationships with loved ones is all evident in the following poems. I have often wondered after having met her and seen a very unique mind at play, how she'd re-enter society after her mountain stint or life phase, how she'd embrace life the way society expects human beings to, and how she'd embrace roles women end up accepting. And it's wonderful to see how she has in her own unique way. And her poems are a window into how her roles aren't binding and her questions haven't stopped. One bit.

Aditya Kripalani

(Award winning filmmaker, writer, musician, and producer.)

Preface

(Written during my Fulbright FLTA tenure. This was the Introduction to my chapbook submission in Writing Poetry with the esteemed American poet Paula Mendoza at the University of Utah, Fall Semester 2018)

Namaste.

Here are some more poems added to the treasury of emotions that this genre has carried over the ages. These poems carry a lot of things, but most prominently- a piece of me, a small town girl from a village Shitlakhet in the Himalayan range of India, lost in this rapidly transforming world.

The themes of the poems are very subjective- bordering on the genre of 'confessional poetry'. My style of writing is usually free verse but my poetry course made me aware of structure and the how and why of poetry forms and the imprints can be found in few of the poems herein. So, these poems are a collage of various moments of my life. I am still not clear about the vision my poetry has or should have, hopefully it will develop over a long period of writing. For now, I am just writing as and when any inspiration hits me.

Poetry remains for me an escape route. Few of these poems are pure momentary expressions inspired by a picture I took or a memory that flashed. I somehow feel like a very Wordsworthian kind of poet who gets an emotion when I encounter something powerful, be it a personal experience recollected after a distance in time or a beautiful scene that inspired me to write and then gets back to the pictures that inspired it.

The editing part of these poems is the biggest challenge for me. The more I try to fit what I have learnt in terms of spacing and highlighting and musicality in my poems, the more I feel estranged. But, on days when we tried to reduce the verbs and adjectives, it was exhilarating. I liked the compact product in my hands. So, I don't know how and when to stop editing and when I am in the process, there's a point I reach when I no longer recognize the authentic emotion behind that piece by reading it aloud and that dampens my spirits and I go back to not editing the next piece till I encounter another which just looks like a scribble and I edit it a little and it shines.

What I want to say here, since it sounds so confusing to me as well, is that- I am on my way. Yay me! I have just embarked on this magical journey and trying out the spells randomly- hopefully one day I will get the drift of saying 'LeviOsa', not 'LevioSA'.

As always, I am lost. That's a perennial feeling I am afraid. (Often on the verge of introducing myself to people with the greeting- "Hello, I am L… L… L… Lost. And you?) I am a novice in this field and much more at ease with prose than poetry, but I want to do more in this. The power and catharsis in poetry is greater than a long prose piece and I want to step higher in the level of craft. I guess it will happen eventually. When it does, I would like to self publish a small collection of poetry and not submit them to a journal.

Submissions and journals make me jittery. My hereditary anxiety goes haywire by the mere thought of doing it, so self publishing seems much easier. Also, I am not sure I want these poems to have a global audience, rather, I would be happy to circulate them clubbed with my Hindi compositions in my close circle of friends, and that would be enough. Maybe.

As I mentioned earlier- just pieces of me.

*2023 edit: Shout out to Major Sidharth Jatana for being the perfect edit in my life. I love you.

Thank you my big shot friend Aditya and Neelu ma'am for taking out time to go through this heap and writing the Foreward and Introduction. Your humility is awe-inspiring.

Introduction

"The truth was a mirror in the hands of God. It fell, and broke into pieces. Everybody took a piece of it, and they looked at it and thought they had the truth."- Rumi

At the very outset, let me start with a disclaimer: "Let not that title befool you!"

The poet might call it a chapbook, but it's actually an anthology...An anthology of intricate emotions, simplified dreams, exasperating crossroads, stupendous happiness, debilitating anxiety, certainty of loss, abridged joy, appropriated lives, parallel universes. Enriched with a happy marriage of Roman and Devanagari, it is a tapestry of exploration and expression of technique and personal limits. Browsing through the poems you'll be a blissful child at times, then an adult befuddled by a mystifying dead-end, then a loving woman enamoured by the idea of love and yet also one who has been through the perils of every underpinning convolutedness of treacherousdeceit. It is contemporary and ancient, vocal and silent, like an eclectic playlist of songs on shuffle which has a Pink Floyd followed by a Jagjeet Singh *gazal* followed by a folk song that turns to a pop ballad, all in equalmeasure.

Creation, of art, as such, is an isolating process for its creator. The dichotomy of the process intensifies because, the creator, who has articulated their vulnerabilities through theirmedia, in seclusion, also then exposes it to their audience. While the poet marks theirclaim onthese momentsof personal recall of their intimacies and interactions with the universe; the reader having been through something similar, also becomes a stake holder of that expression. The artist's human experiences thus, are as universal as they're personal, the reader beseeches presence in the moments that the poet calls their own...

The subliminal spaces that Vandana creates for her reader, allows them to let her words seep in and own them. Till they know they have felt the living and the dying. The stillness and the chaos. One moment to be exalted and then plumet to the depth of the abyss. You'll find political opinions and autobiographic snap shots nestled together with latent memories and generational curses, picturesque and stark all at once! You'll get screamed at with the exact meaning and remain challenged to find the same for the untranslatable. These are what you have qualified for too, sanctions and allowances. So you'll feel the grief and joy, challenge and ease of her life and that's what you'll take away from your experience of partaking from this chapbook.

All I would like to add is, "Let her!" for it's as much yours as it's Vandana's. Her Pieces are yours too.

Perhaps like Rumi would have said, *"We are the mirror – As well as the face in it."*

-Neelu Raut

Friend. Human. Artist. Learner.

(Doesn't identify with any of her posts or appointments. In Pratyāhāra.)

Contents

Dye me white

Three times a week,
sometimes more
if it gets too cold,
I die.
So, when I am dying...

...color me
black n white.
Blacks by you
on the white of me
and pray, make a bookmark
of it and behind a bookshelf
stuck with the wall and never to move
with two clandestine spiders, hide me well.

And just like that,
in the bookstore-
in pieces by you
of me,
touched with tears,
leaving spots on the wall,
let me lie.

Anna

She looks at you-
wondering if you would jump too...?
Fallen in love and yet never truly loved...
After years of that desperate jump.
Thinking about the love that was never hers-
and her husband whom she couldn't love.
She looks at you-
lying in pieces on that railway track still.
Waiting to be complete someday.
Not to be accepted-
Fuck that shit.
No.
Waiting for you to bare it all,
and fuck whoever you want,
slap the teasers and kick the molesters---
She looks at you-
and hopes you would do it one day...

Fight for your Vronsky,
Kill your husbands if need be,
Take Annie and Seryozha,
go to a new city,
start over.
Do anything-
Fuck everyone.

Her slanted, pointed eyes stare at you,
Jumping off from the book cover-
Scream at you, silently and ask-
Would you kill everyone and live-
or, would you jump too?

धुँध

है ऐसी की अब छटती ही नहीं।
कोहरा है ऐसा...
गाड़ियों के बिना
भी फैले जाता है।
जो जो दुबके थे
अपने बिलों में,
वो खाँस-खाँस कर
बाहर निकलें हैं,
बौराए हुए से,
कोहरे में खो रहे हैं।

जो निकले थे
मंज़िल की तलाश में,
वो धुँध में गोल-गोल
घूमे जा रहे हैं।
पथरीली सी आँखें हैं,
रिसती भी नहीं।
धुँध और कोहरा समा गया
आँखों कानों में ऐसे
अब कुछ सुनता दिखता भी नहीं...

शुक्र है वैसे...
कितना कुछ लुट चुका है,
ये पूरा हिसाब ही नहीं।
सबकुछ याद ही नहीं... धुँध
है ऐसी की अब छटती ही नहीं।

The one who is a black dog

I came running away from a
new survey of unsafeness unwalkableness unliveableness,

which showed us degenerated- a disability viral for
selective humans with hymens and lips

to an old one where I was sure the right ticks will give me immunity--
Where people don't rip you open like the blow up dolls
burst open and lie in shreds swept from hellholes once a year.

Funny how just the dogs in the streets got prettier.
Each anew, a sample from a rare breed, especially

the black one who growls at me.

Just like him on my street back home, who was put down
unlike *Golu devju* who followed me across the borders till I was bit and slept.

Here. Never. Ever

She laughs and often takes
me out touches my tummy
and makes me fly
    You mad?.   i stop, fall and shout
    She never existed!   bleed,
howl and cry crawl to my room, fly
high
she returns and i again smile
and laugh… she hides in my
belly- very shy
she is angelic- just like her photograph.

Mefipristone- the word stops
in my mouth another pill goes in
don't you try!
    blob of blood i vomit a dark cloud.
    She's dead,   she flies in
the red sky. his scrubs has bloodstains
that he will deny
he pushes her and I die in
half craving to hold her in
eternity, I sigh
she always smiles- just like her photograph.

She flies often and around-
i trace her hues in the dark, a butterfly
repair the lights she makes no sound,
wake up! dances, glows and

mystifies- in dark. i follow her tracks
and cry!
murmur her name to every plant-
repeat it like
a *mannat* and glorify.
She looks divine- just like her photograph.

It's dark and nobody is home
except tens of hers and
one mother- me.

Except that we don't have a home- neither her, nor him or me.

Within

Yes, I hide.
It's a habit now.
Emily taught me early on.
The little bird died too early.
And that descent was rapid-
and the plank broke too soon.
Too soon did the failure begin,
and joy died,
shrieking in its cradle.
Too soon did the dreams defer-
never got a chance.
And my hiding place gets cozier:
a desert, a forest-
a book, a poem, a photo, a sketch...
My mother, and your eyes.
Your camera can't pierce the cocoon.
It's too deep and dark here
and the lights are bright.
You are too white
and I can't stand that too---
So, just like that-

Scared and hurried-
Shaken, ashamed,
shy and broken.
As is my habit,
I hide.

Every. Few

For every soul is trapped-
but not each gets an escape...

For each heart bleeds-
But not each recieves love...

For each eye sees-
but rarely do they dream...

And when she escapes and loves and dreams-
then...
only then-
caressing her scars-
she understands why only few dare.

रंग

बरसों बाद मिला मुझसे वो पुराना दोस्त मेरा,
रंगरेज़ मेरा।
पर ये क्या?
उसको देखा तो पलकें झुक गयीं,
मेरी बेरंगत मुझको ही अचानक चुभ गयी।

अपने सफ़ेद लबादे जो मैं फ़ख़्र से ओढ़ रही थी,
सादगी नहीं, कफ़न से लगने लगे,
रंगरेज़ की एक झलक ने क्या-क्या दिखा दिया...

नज़रें तो ना उठीं फिर उसके सामने,
पर दो आँसूँ ढुलक पड़े,
उसने उन्हीं को झट से हथेली पर लिया,
और रंगों का एक समुंदर सा बना दिया...
प्रीतम जिस आग के गोले को समुंदर के हवाले कर आयी थीं,
उसने उसी आग की लपटों को,
लाल और नारंगी और पीले को-
नीले और सफ़ेद के साथ मिला दिया,
और दो बेरंग पानी की बूँदों से
रंगों का एक सैलाब सा ला दिया....

मैं वहीं गिर पड़ी,

उस रंगों के उफनते सैलाब को कहाँ रखती?

जैसे-तैसे पलकें उठायीं,

देखा उसे,

तो एक हँसी के ठहाके के साथ उछाल दिया उसने अपने हाथों का वो समुंदर!

सब कुछ रंग गया,

मैं, मेरी परछाई, मेरी ज़मीन, मेरी हवा...

और उन रंगों में घुल कर आ गयी है उसकी हँसी की खनक भी...

जिसे बुनती हूँ मैं,

दिन रात-

मुस्कुराते रंगीन सपनों में,

कुछ लफ़्ज़ों में...

Eulogy

Of the fallen and the sideswept-
There's a eulogy to be made.
No hopes of resurrection, you say?
But a call is yet to be made...
To be made is a wreath of flowers
and be put with the ones that fell.
Of their beauty and sublimity-
Tales the young ones may then tell.
No bonfire of these dreams I pray,
Remember the girls clicking them yesterday?
Holding bunches of them to their bosom,
In messages to the lovers they forever stay.
Immortal are the ones that the wind claimed-
And they are yet not to be swept away.
They are the stuff of dreams that forever stay.
Don't just burn or bury them, I pray... Instead,
Let them fall where they may...
And maybe... the bicycles parked below them-
will carry the fallen ones to a flower heaven far, far away.

Loss. noun.

/lɑːs/

1. Emotionally: A pain immeasurable. Dictionaries and gurus and yogis can't define or understand. A punishment of being human, all too human.

2. Physically: A severed limb. Like all your nerve endings are stumped and blood flow has jammed. Like your brain is only receiving and giving pain. A cyclical rerun of pain churning over and over again.

3. Psychologically: A nightmare you can't wake up from. A limbo where your mind is stuck on an oscillating pendulum, and the hypnosis isn't breaking.

Free

I am not free.
I am not.
Independent nation, yes it is.
Happy nation?
I think not.
Free thinking?
Traditionally trapped.
Free love?
Locked and Banned.
Free expressions?
Shhhhhhh.... Jail's not far.
It is Modi's Raj.
Free religion?
Lol!
Free movement?
Not at night, not with a skirt, no.
Free education?
Parents die of loans.
Free health?
Private practice is all you get.
Free schooling?
You are fed stones.
Yes, we are free.
Because the force guards us.
Yes, we live-

coz soldiers die each night.
Is my sleep free?
No.
It owes death a soldier.
The politicians won't know.
The Independence Day celebrations carry on.
The flag shines bright-
like the tears in my eyes-
For the ones awake in Siachin.
For the ones dead on the hills.
For the ones with a faulty aircraft.
For the ones marching on.
For the ones away on their anniversaries,
For the wives left with a uniform.
For the kids who never knew their hero.
For an India which never gets free.

No. I will not lie.
I am not free.
Freedom is a dream.
of peace on the borders
soldiers having long lives
sacrifices being valued
women being safe
expression being free.
religion being just data.
caste being past.

just being happy-
why is that so hard?

The golden bird is getting dull.
Let's clear some smoke,
let's clear some roads,
let's break some stones,
break the chains,
let her fly-
Till she shines in the golden sky.

भीगी सी नज़्म

कुछ दिनों से सांसें कुछ रुकी रुकी सी हैं-
एक नज़्म लिख रही थी जब ये फूल मिले थे तुम्हारे...
जब ४४ भाई रुख्सत हुए थे हमारे,
एक नज़्म है भीगी भीगी सी आज भी,
हर लफ़्ज़ में कुछ पानी सा है,
अधूरी नहीं है-
मुकम्मल है आधे अल्फ़ाज़ों में भी...
दर्द है कई माओं का उसमें,
कई बहनों की राखियों के धागे भी पिरोए हैं,
पापा की डाँटों की स्याही भी मिलायी है,
भाई से खेली वो आधी शतरंज की बाज़ी भी- .

सोचा था बहुत ख़ूबसूरत नज़्म लिखूँगी,
इन फूलों सरीखी एक ताबीर बुनूँगी...
पर हर ख़याल पर कुछ बादल आए,
हर लफ़्ज़ पर एक बूँद टपकी,
सारी सियाही मेरी रुमाल पर ही रुक गयी है।
सामने है नज़्म मेरी भीगी भीगी सी,

तुम्हारी तस्वीर भी है धुँधली धुँधली सी,
ख़ाकी रंग का धुआँ सा है,
और मेरी सांसें भी हैं-
रुकी रुकी सी।

कुछ-कुछ

क्यूँकि पूरा नहीं दे सकती,
सारी जो हूँ मैं-
सहमी सी, घबरायी सी
सबको सुलझाती हुयी,
ख़ुद को उलझायी सी...

वो मैं बस अपने लिए ही हूँ-
एक थमे हुए बवंडर की तरह,
अपने सारे चेहरे सम्भाले हुए,
मैं जी रही हूँ
सब कुछ लिपटाए हुए।

तो तुम्हें मैं क्या दूँ?
कैसे दे दूँ?
सम्भालोगे कैसे तुम?
मेरा इतना सारा सब कुछ...?

पर क़ुछ तो है तुम्हारा हक़-
हाँ...
मेरे पचास चेहरों में से

वो फेरों वाला,
और भी दो-चार चेहरे तुम्हारे।
ये है मेरा क़ुछ,
तुम्हारी क़ुछ साँसों के नाम।

और ऐसे ही बस,
मेरे सब में से थोड़ा सा क़ुछ-
तुम्हारा,
और तुम्हारा, मेरा..

क़ुछ-क़ुछ होता है बहुत-क़ुछ वैसे...
पर ना भी हुआ तो-
क़ुछ-ना-क़ुछ तो होगा ही
काफ़ी-
जीने के लिए।

Closed Door

The closed door is a silence I love.
The unsaid and the unheard live together there.
An uncomposed symphony plays there all day long...
I hear the guffaws and sobbings too in turn.
I sit there long before the closed door and hear the unheard-
I dream of places unknown and people unmet-
The closed door holds all other doors.
Oh, the closed door knows them all...

Decorated

I am stuck-
so deep,
with so many labels-
I bleed inside.

But you like it, don't you?
Putting your expectations on me?
and to make sure they stick-
you drive them in with a thumb-pin.

You don't like my whiteness,
all corners you color of your choice.
You won't give me any space-
your words and quotes fill me all!

You want me to be pretty and colourful,
full of knowledge and heavy sounding words-
be something to be proud.
To fetch you awards.

I bleed, you know.
With your quotes and your colors,
your dreams and deadlines-
I fall every second day!
I am merely dust crumbling inside,
you stuck too many pins...
and nothing you now do,
can keep me as one.

I just wanna be blank-
undo all you ever did,
go back to being a log...
Try remembering- for once?

what it was to just-
breathe.

-Yours,
beautifully decorated,
Notice Board.

Teens together.

not your todays
not this adult
who understands all-
no…
show me your yesterdays-
maybe-
your crazy teens?

your adult perfection
is scary
i often feel small
so, would you please-
show me your teens?
show me your screams
swears
pimpled skin
and weird hairdos.

you eat all now-
gimme a peek
in your tantrum
with a broken plate
and you crying.
what did your mom do?
a slap?
chappal?

or a warning?
that story would be really good too!

slowing over speed breakers-
dear…
that just won't do.
take me to a time
when you didn't care-
flying your bike over them,
you ruled them,
not them you.
tell me how you fell,
how you came home drunk-
and maybe about the
dirty home scene later?

not prim,
not proper,
not in starched olive greens.
show me a grinning you,
a cig between your lips
in a hoodie
with improper captions
and faded torn jeans.

let's scream
giggle
break all rules
run wild
together?
be teens together?
wouldn't that be
so much better?

बेनाम

श्रिंगार जड़ित कविता नहीं,
लोकगीत सरीखी कहानी है हमारी-
बेनाम, बेबाक़...

कोई पूछे किसने लिखी?
कब लिखी?
तो मैं हँस कर बोलूँ-
सबने, सदियों से...

earth-y

fallen leaves
crawling animals
washed up objects-
poems hiding in sight
earth cradles all
and puts a rhythm on them-
a soft wind plays the flute,
a lizard slithers smoothly by,
a wave splashes up one on the shore-
oh... the sounds of these things,
the hustle and rustle and bustle
of leaves, shells, animals and things making music
for the eyes to hear
and the fingers to see...
earth cradling them all,
and slowly letting me peek.

My opaque glasses

are weirdly put on my nose,
I am told.
They are always there
as I look at the darkness
as I walk and talk.

They told me
I speak from just one side.
I agree this time.
My opaque glasses sit there.
And I drown in darkness.
And I can’t see two
sides of the cheap coin.

Oh...
but with your crystal clear lenses,
you are in the dark too.
you talk one sided too.
Are you me too?
Am I you too?
These cracked, broken glasses

are mine
and yours, too?
Maybe just like Samson,
our eyes are cut out too.

Wondering

where the colors fell
off me...? .

Somewhere on my way from
school
that red spot
on my Saturday skirt
reminding me
I can get pregnant-
I lost my colors.
Between that boy
whose words were
just the size I found him
insufficient-
gone too far too soon
and the flimsy ring
that traps my bloodflow-
I lost my colors.
On that bus to Jaipur
and uncle ji
grazing my innards
and the friend who
hugged me with a tent
in his pants-
lost my colors.

From the moment my
bleeding started
till my heart stops-
I lose my colors.
Flowers all-
Butterflies all-
Girls all-
Drooping, dying all-
resignated, raped all-
Unsafe all-
Molested all-
Wait-
Five minutes please.... .
Will paint them pink.
Just the way you want.
Don't you wonder anymore
where my colors fell?
Cuts and scratches-
made by the handsome
and not-so
you alls.

ज़रूरी हैं क्या?

ज़रूरी है क्या?
कुछ बनना,
किसी की शान बनना,
किसी के जैसा बनना,
किसी का बनना?

ज़रूरी है क्या?
ऊपर पहुँचना,
थोड़ा सा और ऊपर पहुँचना,
उनसे ऊपर पहुँचना,
सबसे ऊपर पहुँचना,
फिर वहीं रुके रहना?

ज़रूरी है क्या?
दौड़ना,
और तेज़ दौड़ना,
सबको पीछे छोड़,
आगे पहुँचना,
सबसे पहले पहुँचना?

थकते नहीं हो तुम क्या?
सबको? सबको हरा पाओगे? वाक़ई?
सुनो… रुको ज़रा,
साँस तो लो-
उसको जी भर के देख तो लो…!

सोचो तो ज़रा... सच में,
सबसे तेज, सबसे ऊपर, सबसे बेहतर होना-
ज़रूरी है क्या?

Some evenings

I burn slowly
drop by drop
bone by bone
my veins carry the lava
all through my body
scalding everything
I thought was mine
lungs, kidney, liver
heart- and there it burns
aflame!
Not at once- no
simmering there
while my walls and valves
too burn-
ventricle by ventricle
a wildfire spreading
in the undergrowth
of the dermis
purging me once
and all
for the pyre that
wouldn't otherwise
even burn
as my tears
stop all fire

that I step on
to clean me
of you. Off you. .

So, some evenings-
Hades pities me
lends me his fire
so I burn-
drop by drop
bone by bone
and walk aflame-
dripping blood
while you-
Burn.

Walking tall.

with the cut hand
in the broken phone
ripped screen
that keeps your sharpnels
running through my channels
with the dirty Ganges water
Ma made me swallow
corruption in my soul
I see as your shadow
overlaps mine
the smelly tiffin I had to clean
but didn't. Couldn't.
Won't.
Shon't
Mon't.
Ton't.
Fon't.
Hon't.
And the limping leg
that carries me away
but not afar- nearest to you-
or him. Not her.
The scalp swelling
in the phone carrying my hand

bleeding sharpnels
and a montage of smelly delusions.

Walking tall.
Dripping shadows.

Insomniac

what's worse-
you fly over
and don't even bother
that I ain't in your area
or that you search
for a tiny hand waving at you;
that you smile at my mails
or cry on video calls; that
you realize it might disappear
and tremble or you know it
will survive and await? Is it
the strength that kills or
the wait? Is it your hand
that pulls me from this abyss
or your pain that pushes
me there? Does your
love keep me sane or
your memories that
make me
an insomniac?

Sham

Darling... Don't be dead.
Not just yet.

You whisper in my ears
as I hit the bottom -
in a lonely room with pending deadlines
and no desire to finish them.
With three incomplete serious poems
and your picture on the table.
I try to write, wash my face
and see myself in the mirror,
sans the foundation
and the filters
and the happiness I paste on.
It's spotty and brown
so I pick up a knife and spade
scrape away the dirt and their touches-
and start digging up all the spots
while counting the meter in each line
making it more sonoric-
remove the yellows and the browns
and epidermal thingy and the flesh thingy
till I reach my bones.
Seven red pits on each side now
with some white finally.

I see my bones
that you kissed.
And the pitholes-faced me smiles
and as I pick up the knife
put the poems aside,
and go downwards,
towards my neck that you so love.

Just when I hear you say-
Darling... Don't be dead.
Not just yet.

(P.S::: I reply with my hollow eyes---
I already am-
We live a sham.)

The leather belt

Wipe a lone tear away-
when you hear him sing
the tune and instrument
stuck in your head-
once in your arm.
Stroke the cut in your thigh
and scribble with rust-
wake up late for class,
bunk-
Reread the dried blood,
fire it up- literally.

Hate your words,
cry a little,
make a poster- hate it.
Make a fool of yourself-
again.
Invite people who never come,
look in the mirror-
hate your face,
scratch your pimples
and then howl with the pain
and-
hate yourself enough...

to know it's time
to conjure him up
everywhere-
to see him-
roll him up in a joint
to smoke up by your bones
and exorcise
(last evening's poetry,
the leather belt)
the bones full of self pity
and screaming with hate—
of exhumed mummies
rolled up stylishly
in the joint that he is.

Stuck

I want to pluck you by your cheeks, the cheeks cleared of the structure, with a little highlight, less shadows and no sharpness at all. I want to pull you by your cheeks and then stick you on to these marks my life has left and your filter has removed and though you who changes from Nostalgia to Valencia to Inkwell- are always pretty and loved by people here, remember that I can delete you, but you not me and now, what do you say about being stuck on to my flesh, han??? I will administer good anesthesia, you will be so drunk, that you will glow while you stick with that high look on my low, dull skin. Don't worry... nobody will notice any of us missing or us fused or anything new. They usually don't, do they? Till you shoot someone. Then they do. I do.

Her

No. I am not okay.
She is here, again.
She was away for a while
while I partied and smiled.
But something called her back
last night,
she came to keep me safe
from a 37 years old man
with white shoes. Now
he is locked safely away while
she sleeps with me in bed
with lights shut off and tells me
it is dark outside.
I can't go check too.
Gagged and chained-
you know her, don't you?

Canvas-sing

The way I see it, it would get tired of its colorlessness and the wait for an artist, and call upon some dirty finger to at least touch it, color it somehow.

I am a girl, I know this.

ख़्वाहिश

यूँ ही नहीं जाते बाहिर मेरी ज़ां
की बस सोचा और निकल गए...

ये जो जगमग सी दुनिया है ना,
बस ख्वाहिश में है तुम्हारी...

तो सम्भालो अपनी चादर भले से,
अपनी पलकें उठाना जरा संभल के...

मुस्कुराना तो और भी रुक-रुक के.
और चलना ज़रा हौले-हौले...

क्यूँकि ये जो दुनिया है ना,
बस ख़्वाहिश में है तुम्हारी।

Black

My color-
purple
rains after ages-
dissolves my blues
in fiery sunsets,
howling goodbyes,
and crimson
and paints my flesh
anew.

In the canyons
your touch made
there are rivers
of purple
amidst bleak
landscapes
of wilting
brown sunflowers
and
fake pink ones.

My color-
purple
rains after ages
painting the white city
Black.

Whoop

That mutilated face
In the park
the screaming,
the hands,
the face,
the distortion and
then this child's whoop.

I hold on,
mimic a smile
and return home
and find her there-
everywhere.
I blink, she doesn't.
I touch her, she's cold,
immobile.

I turn and see clawmarks
she smiles, turning
with me.
I want to strangle her,
mutate her,
burn her!
but
she dies only with
me.

A smirk, a victory.
Burn the Munichs,
capture the whoop
smile till it hurts, she
says
and burns holes
in my facade.
There's a crack
in the dark
and she is me.

again.

Un- said/heard/seen.

Flying in the clouds,
you sway in your pride.
dressed up as an officer-
you forget your crime.
I stare at the spot on the
carpet and see it melting away.
The world gets fluid often and
my tongue numb saying
I am fine, thank you.
It's haunting without you,
I float usually, unable to walk
in a state of curfew.

You write some alphabets-
sometimes you do. I don't say
you don't love me, maybe you do.
I see the shapes and the word
love, and even reply. But there's
a song which my lips want
to sing to yours and see you
smile and kiss me while I cry
away the words unsaid and
beg me to not be so sad.
It's your touch that completes
the song, you usually complete

them all! And it's funny how
you still don't know.
The flimsy alphabet can't, don't,
won't do it. Oh no, it won't.
The designs I want to sing-
your ears they won't reach,
amorphous, they won't be
a poem too, and suffocated
in my heart- they die cold.

The wait seems to spin itself
from the silk of my sorrows,
and makes a porous blanket
keeping me covered with you,
yet always cold. I do smile
all day long, but it gets
impossible to breathe.
Fly here, it's a cold bed.
Or, just hear the unsaid,
grieve the unfallen tears
bury my coffin and finally
at peace-
I leave
. . . . . . unseen.

Wait

It's official,
this is forever.
I hear the congratulations
cut the cake and cry aside.
The joy is for real now,
one wait is over, and
I wear his ring.
And so I carry in my heart-
the misery too of another wait.
My lips carry his buttersoft kisses,
my body remembers them too well-
he is my mate, my fate.
Life now seems a charade
that I often just hate!

Everything is hauntingly same-
nothing changed...
His face is planted everywhere I go.
I see him in small kids
in lifeless autumn leaves,
in the burning yellow trees
in fiery sunsets behind churches
and in everybody on the streets.
He is part Jesus
and a little of Radha too. He is

in the glass of wine I miss
and the Tequila shots we took.
No. It's not him I miss,
it's my life I do.
It's not the distance that kills,
It's the broken Aladdin ka chirag which does.
and Buckbeak who doesn't fly me to him.

Coz all I need is a pint of magic and/or his kiss.

Hands.

Hands are meant be held.
Funny.
Funny how eating a chocolate
can turn a tragedy too.
Damn your vampirish love-
sucking me of the little life I had,
leftover joy hidden from Emily and Sylvia-
my secret pills that I relished.
Damn you for devouring them too.
Hands are meant to be held. You hear?
Mine crack and bleed from scratches.

Don't you dare laugh.
It ain't funny anymore.
My cold, cracked hands just touched
a picture of you. And
they dropped off and fell.
It's better now.
A little absurd without my hands, yes.
But, no hands are better than empty ones.

Hands are meant to be held.
Funny-
how dark a dark chocolate can make me.
Dark and handless.
All sweet things be damned now.
So, damn you.

Away.

The sun too high,
the yellow grassland caught fire
and the cozy cottages collapsed.
A cool breeze came,
the wooden silhouette emerged
and dense deodars grew from my palm.

Chilgozas of Chilianaula

Chiliyanaula-
and my nani's home.
a romantic tale-
of milking the cows,
dirtying your clothes.
three dresses a day,
and still be dirty always.
of eating chips in secret,
and begging *bhai* for Coke

Of playing on the slopes,
of holes in frocks,
torn shoes
lost socks-
and getting scolded
round the clock.
Of mama making
us do army drills,
of visiting the canteen
of walking to Ranikhet-
looking for *chilgoze*
in pinecones!
It's a long way home...

These pretty, empty cones
remind me everyday
this is not home.
Because where I am from-
there are always
people without earphones,
ammas, bubus and nantinas
with their incessant talks
laughing and singing
on rounding hillslopes
looking for treasures-
chilgoze
in large, heart shaped pinecones.

Moments.

I put a pin
on the wall
yesterday-
Wanting your face
in my room.
Shining golden-
the thumb pin
stuck on my finger,
matching
your ring.
Exactly like
your nose tip
that I press...
smooth round
and cold.

It never did
stay there but.
I hammered it in
and hurt
my little finger.
But it fell-
again
and
again

and
again...

Unlike your memories
stuck
in my head.

They stay put.
always.

I try
not to miss you.
to untangle my fingers
and let you go,
let myself breathe,
Too pointed
these moments-
and stuck too deep.

Headless.

The slain one lay in tatters-
Thrown on the road oft travelled.
Dusty and muddy and spat upon.
One day in the bed in warm innocence-
another day beheaded in the street.

Headless but clothed.
Cut, but unbled.

Unlike the little girls found in the ditches.
Headed but naked.
Cut and bleeding.
One day in the bed in warm innocence-
Another day raped in the street. .

An untold story-
An unpunished crime.
The beheaded can't rise,
won't get back on the display shelf.
The family won't kiss and hug it again...

The raped babies too.
No home with dignity.
Muted and murdered.
No hugs and no kisses.
No love to be ever had.

Just objects to be clicked headless.
Faces a mosaic.
And made news of.
And a horror in their dead eyes.

What a world for dolls and babies.
Marvel.
What a Marvel.

Insane

What better place to write than the red one o'clock room?
a little away from midnight gloom—-

The distance from midnight makes me recover
keeping me sane.
I get time to adjust and reshape my masks
put on my tinted lip balm to meet you again...
And in your messed up laboratory
our jackets packed in smoke,
my scribblings lie open, bleeding, and prone...
I try to stitch them with painted cheeks
a new me I feel, just when…

you turn, stare blank at my bloody hands
and murmur how I appear to you-
as you to me
this world too-
Insane.
I hear you
And the world echoes-
'insane'.

Carpe Diem

Of falling leaves, fading youth and the promise of spring-
Who knows more than the person on a cliff?
Of frivolous February that just passed-
She tells tales to the miseries of March.

Of burning books and running ink-
There's a tale yet to be told...
Of unkept evenings and unruly nights-
There are confessions yet to be made.
But then... She sighs and crushes the dry and broken leaves.
On these fallen objects of destiny she vents.
And clicking a picture of that moment-
Already history- she repeats the bag's dictum-
Carpe Diem.

Lingering

There are days of darkness dear.
days of bone cold frights.
There are moments when I see me dead,
And, alas... you don't cry.

There are days of doubts darling.
There are moments of misery.
There are moments I want to kill you myself,
And do away with any mockery.

Death tempts me in turns.
Somenights more, somedays less.
You make me fly high my love.
The air carries me to a pit too.

I become a mess.
Me. Moments. Misery. Mockery.
The darkness defines.
The darkness devours.

There's a dark home it seems.
In shadows I hide...
In the dimming candle light sometimes,
You linger.

अधूरा

और बस यूँ ही सब चले गए,
उस नज़्म को आधा सुना छोड़ कर,
उस बचे हुए जाम को प्याले के हवाले कर,
एक क़िस्से को उनकहा ही छोड़ कर,
एक हँसी को होंठों में समेट कर,
सब आधा अधूरा छोड़ सब चले गए...

सिवाय मेरे अकेलेपन के-
वो जितना आया था ना शाम के साथ,
उतना ही रहा.

बाक़ी सब आधा,
बस वो पूरा-
शाम दर शाम,
रात दर रात.

9 789357 411998

Printed by Libri Plureos GmbH in Hamburg, Germany